All for Ben

First published 1986 by Walker Books Ltd,
184-192 Drummond Street, London NW1 3HP

© 1986 Helen Craig

First printed 1986
Printed and bound by L.E.G.O., Vicenza, Italy

British Library Cataloguing in Publication Data
Craig, Helen
A welcome for Annie.–
(The Susie and Alfred books)
I. Title   II. Series
823'.914[J]   PZ7
ISBN 0-7445-0264-0

SUSIE AND ALFRED

· IN ·

A WELCOME FOR
❖ ANNIE ❖

· HELEN CRAIG ·

WALKER BOOKS
LONDON

Susie was at Alfred's house watching
the new family move in next door.

There were Mr and Mrs Jones, Baby Fred
and a girl called Annie. Annie was a
little shy and did not dare to look
at Alfred and Susie.

'She's not very friendly,' said Susie.
'She didn't even look our way.' They
decided right there and then that
they did not like Annie.

Alfred's mother, Mrs Plum, came out and
invited Mr and Mrs Jones and their children
to tea the next day. 'Susie and Alfred will
simply love playing with Annie,' she said.

'Now you must both be nice to Annie
and make her welcome,' said Mrs Plum.
Susie and Alfred were not very pleased.

'How can we welcome someone we don't even like?' they grumbled. But Mrs Plum would not listen. So they put their heads together to plan a welcome for Annie.

Next day they started early. 'Please, Mother,
can I have some water?' asked Alfred.
'Help yourself,' said his mother. 'I'm busy right now.'

'Can we borrow these blankets and my old
    raincoat?' Susie asked.
'Certainly,' said her mother without looking up.

By lunch-time they had almost finished.

After lunch Mrs Trot came to help Mrs Plum
prepare the tea. 'What are you two so busy at?'
Mrs Trot asked.
'Just making a welcome for Annie,' Susie
answered sweetly.

'What nice, well brought-up children we have,'
their mothers said proudly to each other.

At last it was tea-time. The doorbell rang.
'Do come in,' said Mrs Plum to all the Joneses.

While the others sat down at the table, Mrs Plum
took Annie out to Susie and Alfred.
'You can have your tea in the garden,' she said.

'Hello, Annie,' said Susie in her nicest voice.
'We've built you a welcome – do come in!'

Annie looked at the welcome. She looked
and looked. 'After one of you,' she said.
'Oh no,' said Susie. 'You first.'

'After one of you,' said Annie stubbornly.
'But it's your welcome,' said Alfred. 'You
    must go in first.'

But Annie stood firm and refused to budge
while Susie and Alfred tried their best
to persuade her to go in first.

The grown-ups were busy having tea. Susie
and Alfred were busy arguing with Annie.
No one noticed Baby Fred.

Ohhhhhhhhhhhh!

Baby Fred made such a noise that everyone
came running. 'Oh, our poor baby!' cried
Mr and Mrs Jones.
'Oh, Alfred! Oh, Susie! How could you?'
cried Mrs Plum and Mrs Trot together.

Susie and Alfred mumbled something about
it all being a mistake and how sorry they were.
But Annie was smiling.

Baby Fred was not hurt, just a bit wet. His father
took him indoors to dry out.
'I think I'm going to like living here,' said Annie.

'Would you like to help me welcome my cousin
Cedric when he visits next week?' Annie asked.
'Yes! Yes!' cried Susie and Alfred, beginning to
like Annie very much indeed.